Passages

An Anthology

by

Pakefield Writing Group

Passages

©Pakefield Writing Group 2022

ISBN 9798365927353

All rights reserved. No part of this publication may be reproduced, distributed or transmitted in any form or by any means, including photocopying, recording or other electronic or mechanical methods, without the prior written permission of the publisher, except in cases of brief quotations embodied in critical reviews and certain other non-commercial uses permitted by copyright law.

Pakefield Writing Group has asserted its right under the Copyright, Designs and Patents Act, 1988, to be identified as the author of this work.

A catalogue record of this book is available from the British Library

Acknowledgements

Jo Wilde, our wonderful editor and publisher, for painstakingly reading through our offerings, making the necessary adjustments for them to be publicly acceptable, then laying them out in a suitable framework for publication.

Midge Mellor, member of our group, and our co-ordinator and curator, who, with humour and patience, has kept us all on task, and negotiated with the providers of those functions that are outside most of our talents, such as they are, namely the editing, publishing, jacket design and the Foreword.

Di Bettinson, a member of our group, writer and painter, who has so beautifully illustrated some of the stories in a way that somehow matched the imaginations of those of us less artistically gifted.

Harry Quirk, our Foreword writer, who runs the Lowestoft Writers' Guild, for a gracious and thoughtful summary of what this sort of book means to those who pluck up the courage and stir their muses to create and write stories, and to those who might read them.

Our thanks to **Sean Patrick** who worked tirelessly on the book cover illustrations. He designed the wraparound cover to reflect the titles and give small clues to the stories within the book.

Given that he was working with a writer who once drew a cat that everyone thought was an elephant, we think he did an outstanding job.

All profits from the sale of this book are shared between East Anglian Children's Hospice and the PDSA.

Foreword

Despite its romanticism, writing something creative and then being able to share it with the world is incredibly difficult, not just on a practical level but an emotional one as well. For myself, as well as many others, when you're working on something, there are constant thoughts that it's not good enough, or that it will never be seen, so what's the point? It is thoughts like these that prevent many talented people from making that first step towards creativity.

For the most part, writing is a very private practice and writers often forget that there are people, other than themselves, who want to read their work, or that there are people who want to support their craft and support them as creative people. This is why groups like the Pakefield Writing Group are so important in providing an opportunity for writers of all kinds to meet and be writers together. To be published in any way is an immense achievement by any author who is lucky enough to do so. Everyone involved in the making of this book should be incredibly proud of what they have collectively created.

If you are holding this book, and reading these words, thank you. You have played a part in something incredible, the creation of a book and the sharing of stories. You are about to embark on a journey through a diverse collection of short stories that have all been lovingly crafted for these pages.

Take your time, enjoy it, and give the writers of the Pakefield Writing Group your appreciation.

Harry Quirk
Growing Theatre C.I.C
Lowestoft Writers Guild

Contents

Title	Page
Passage of Time	1
A Home on the Rolling Deep	3
Ellie	9
Letter to Sinterklaas	15
Martin	19
Dandelion	25
Mary	31
Seat 41	37
Bus Home	43
Undercurrent	49
Ink	53
Off World	59
Landscapes, Seascapes and Crocodile Rock	65
Trailer Adventures	75
Lucida’s Tale	81
My Grandfather’s Clock	87
Stolen by the Smog	91
Full Circle	101

Passage of Time

by Midge Mellor

Walk a mile in my shoes. Every journey starts with a first step. Travel broadens the mind. So many clichés about the ways and means of getting from here to there. Like putting one foot in front of the other. Or arriving in the nick of time. Plodding along.

What if I don't want to move or think ahead? What if I want to stay exactly where I am?

But I can't hold back time. Seconds have passed since even I **had** that thought. Hours have flown by since you put the ring on my finger. It has already made a little groove on my skin.

Time trips along invisibly.
In a couple of hours, I will be getting on a plane, which I have never done before; going to a place I have never been before; meeting people I have never met before. How will I feel then? Will this journey broaden my mind? How will I change?

The passage of time is undefined.
I have almost forgotten the emotions I felt at my wedding. Already, doubts are eating their way into my psyche. How will my life change? Will I learn? Will I be happy?
Tempus fugit. Time flees.

A Home on the Rolling Deep
by Claire Walker

In the Year of Our Lord 1869 the tea clipper Margarita *set sail from Liverpool, carrying passengers from the industrial towns of Wales to a new life on the unknown shores of Patagonia, at the bottom of the world. As the sails unfurled and the ship headed for the wide-open seas, those aboard were unaware that a stowaway had embarked on an unexpected journey...*

53° 24' N, 3° 00' W - Liverpool

I squeeze and squirm my way through a maze of booted feet and swishing skirts. It's raining hard but still the docks are teeming with people. Colourful curses follow me, as does my pursuer, though he has fallen back, unable to navigate the crowds as fast as I can – not even he would be so stupid as to charge forwards while clutching that vicious knife. All because I stole one measly fish. A cat has to eat, after all. But he didn't see it that way and if he catches me, I'll end up sinking in the filthy depths of the dock or, if that knife is anything to go by, in the cooking pot. Then there's a gap in the forest of legs and I burst through it, up a wooden slope and then down a flight of slippery steps.

All is dim and quiet now; I crawl into a corner and lick my sodden fur. Then more thundering feet, and voices, so many lilting voices.

"Are we doing the right thing, Hugh?"…"I'd rather risk drowning than being buried alive in the pit…""…independence, that's what we want!"…

But no-one comes down here and I relax. I am too nervous to venture out yet, even though the smell down here is rank. I leap into one of the strange pouch-like things that hang from the beams, where I curl up and am rocked to sleep.

49°17' N, 7°07' W

"Out of my hammock, you mangy beast!"

I am wrenched from slumber and only just manage to land on my feet as I'm hurled to the floor. He's massive and grizzled, with hair as orange as mine.

"How did that get in here?" another man says.
"Just chuck it overboard, Billy."
"No." A harsh, growling voice that stops the others short. I am scooped up by a pair of muscled, tattooed arms and I squall and writhe but his grip is too tight to escape.

"Okay, Mr Gallo."
Under his breath Billy adds, "Don't think it's getting any of my rations."
"He can earn his keep."

He? Can't they tell I'm a girl?

"This ship is rife with rats. Let's call him Seaman Sam."
Mr. Gallo strokes my head.
"And Amos will see him right."

39°05′ N, 13°35′ W

Mr Gallo (who for some reason Miss Jones keeps calling Raff) wasn't kidding. Amos the cook is soft as pudding. He slips me morsels meant for the passengers' plates, something Captain Keable had better not find out about. I think the captain likes me, though; he lets me sleep on his chair. I think Miss Morgan likes me too, after I killed a rat in her cabin.
Time passes slowly. Tedium falls upon the ship like a

weighted blanket. The whole world is nothing but blue, and white. Deep blue sea with its frilled white crests, and soaring, shrieking white gulls. Infinite blue sky and billowing white sails under drifting clouds...

20° 38′ N, 20° 57′ W

I am roughly seized by the scruff of my neck and the world tilts as I am swung dizzily through the air to hang suspended above the shining swell. Young Thomas Griffiths is dangling me over the side. My heart is pounding and I want to struggle but I mustn't, I mustn't. Then there's a sudden, sharp movement and his grip slackens. I yowl. But we are both jerked back and as I drop to the deck, limp with relief, I see that Raff has Thomas by the scruff of his neck. Raff is yelling then there's a swift hand movement that leaves Thomas clutching his ear.

0° 05′ S, 33° 19′ W

We have crossed the equator. Apparently this is a big event and the crew celebrates by chucking buckets of water over each other. Some of the passengers are joining in, mostly the men but Mrs Davies and Miss Morgan are there too, and now they have all gone below to get very drunk and generally behave like sailors do when they are ashore.

19° 25′ S, 26° 54′ W

I sense a storm brewing. The air is charged with tension and I feel restless, so I dash from one end of the ship to the other, getting under everyone's feet. The wind is snapping at the sails as the crew scrambles to lower them. The ship pitches and rolls and there are cries of 'Heave-to!' I am pushed below to join the other passengers who cower and vomit miserably in their cabins and there is loud banging as the hatches are nailed shut.

38° 09′ S, 26° 54′ W

When the storm finally passes, we're one hundred miles off course. I hear Billy grumble, "That's what you get for bringing women aboard."
By the look on her face I think Mrs Davies has overheard him but she is too exhausted and thankful that the storm is over to bother to object.

42° 09′ S, 33° 19′ W - Puerto Madryn, Argentina

"Land ahoy!"
The cry comes from the crow's nest and suddenly the ship is alive with excitement and anticipation and not a small degree of anxiety. I look to the bleak, low-lying shore and wonder what I will do next, but a cat who can survive in Liverpool can survive anywhere. I intend to slink away amidst the general

chaos and I have one paw on the gangplank before I am yet again lifted by those muscled, tattooed arms. “Stop right there, Seaman Sam,” Raff orders. “The crew hasn’t been granted shore leave. You’re staying with us.”

Ellie

by Hilary Lepine

They weren't expecting me. How could they? Fairly ordinary family, going about their business. You don't want me turning up unannounced on your doorstep. How do you get into a state of expectation, of readiness, for someone like me anyway? I suppose some people do give me some thought, but not that many really. Most people have no idea how to handle me, what to say, how to behave. And they're often scared. I don't blame them for that, it's a one-off visit, if you like. Well, normally it is. In this case, it was going to be a bit different.

The Nelsons. Lovely family, the Nelsons. Quite special, in fact. The one I know best is Ellie, seven years old, missing her two top front baby teeth. Black hair, warm brown eyes. Mischievous and enchanting. She has a beautiful soul, which somehow illuminates her from inside. She seems to glow; people can't help being drawn to her. And completely unspoilt. She has a little brother, Tommy, a rascal if ever there was one, mad about football. He's unspoilt too.

Mum's a teacher, and Dad's a police officer. Voices are very rarely raised in this household, and generally speaking, everyone is happy. I could go on about consistency, security, respect, love, but I'm sure you get the picture. I know it sounds too good to be true, but it is the truth.

There they were, on a family day out, Mum, Dad, Tommy and Ellie, making their way to the museum. Out of nowhere, a car came roaring by, mounted the pavement, and hit little Ellie. Then carried on.

You can imagine the scene; I won't go into details. I went over to Ellie.

"Am I dead?" she asked, in that innocent, utterly ingenuous way that children have, as if it was the most natural question in the world.

Ellie looked at me, wide-eyed, out of those soft brown eyes. She sat up, and looked down at her still, prone body, cradled in her mother's arms. I had been sent to her side to escort her through the veil and over the threshold into the Light. Don't ask me how I know who and when to visit – it's just one of those things I KNOW.

"Yes, Ellie. You are," I said, as gently as I could.

Some people think I'm harsh and cruel, but they're mistaken. I do what I do quietly and calmly, and with love, actually. I don't want to scare people. I want them to pass over with peace and contentment.

Even the ones who have been cruel, or dishonest, or even committed terrible crimes. Like that car driver, for example. I'm not here to judge. That's for a Higher Authority, once they get the other side of the Light.

Ellie seemed to know what was going on, as children often do. They're so much more conscious, tuned-in, if you like, than adults. She smiled a gappy, toothless smile, and looked over my shoulder. I knew what she was smiling at. They all do it. It was the Light behind me, luminous and beckoning, like no other Light they have ever seen. I couldn't resist smiling back. Some people have the power to make others feel good, to make the world a better place, and Ellie was one of those.

I held out my hand. She took it in absolute trust. We started to walk slowly toward the Light.

"Will they be alright, Mum, Dad and Tommy? Will I be able to see them sometimes?"
"Ellie, they're going to be very sad for quite a long time. You must keep sending them love to remind them that you're still part of them, and that you're happy where you are."

Ellie turned and waved goodbye to her family and to her physical form with the most radiant smile you've ever seen.

Then I noticed a piece of the Light begin to detach, and come toward us, getting even more brilliant. I knew what it was, of course. I had seen it before – not that often, but often enough. It was an Angel Recall. Then I realised just who it was doing the Recall. This was big. And I mean BIG. It was Archangel Gabriel himself. Ellie was obviously needed on earth for something really important.

Gabriel came right up. To be honest, it's quite hard to see at first in an Angel's brilliance, especially one of the Tops, if you know what I mean. After a while, though, your eyes adjust. But Ellie, she had no problem. She just looked at Gabriel, still smiling.

"Do you mind going back, Ellie?" he asked her. "It might be difficult for you, and your physical body will hurt for a while, but you are making a big difference to a lot of people, and there are things you need to do when you grow up, very important things."
"Do I go back to Mum, Dad and Tommy?"
"Yes, just as you were before."

Ellie's smile changed. She had a little frown, like she was really thinking. She turned and looked at the Light. I could see she was drawn to it and tempted to carry on into it. But I never interfere in these moments. I'm just a peaceful escort for these journeys.

Ellie looked at her family and her body. She looked at Gabriel. She looked at me. You could see the indecision. They're always like that, the ones who have these Recalls, what you call Near Death Experience. It might sound surprising, but actually, it's not an easy decision for a soul to make, because going into the Light is going back to Source, and that's very attractive, of course. Going back to the body can be painful.

Well, anyway, Ellie went for it. That smile lit up her face again. She nodded.
"I'll go back as long as Tommy stops screaming."
Gabriel smiled. He put his hand on her head.
"Bless you, Ellie." A personal blessing from Gabriel. Wow! I knew that she really was special and destined for some great contribution to the world.
"What about Tommy? He's still screaming."
Gabriel laughed. I jest not. The Archangel Gabriel laughed. That's the sort of person Ellie is.
"He'll stop, I promise. Ready?"

Ellie nodded and smiled that gappy smile. She took his hand. She took my hand. Together, we walked away from the Light and back to her family and her body on the pavement.

It's taken me a few minutes to tell you this story, but in real time, all this only lasted a few seconds. That's how it is with these things. I had to leave

Ellie there, of course. It wasn't my job to stay. But I must admit, once I got out of her energy zone, I did stop and watch for a while. Gabriel held her, then gently put her back into her body. She moaned and moved. Her parents - well, I'm sure you can imagine. And Tommy stopped screaming.

Letter to Sinterklaas

by Midge Mellor

Dear St. Nicolas,

I write to you in fond hope that you will be able, in your role as patron saint of archers and global gift giver, to provide some much-needed gifts for my daughter, Marian, and her friends.

They have been helping the poor and dispossessed for many a year, doing what is right and good. Even though they have found themselves on the wrong side of the law many times this year, I trust you will accept their lawlessness was committed with the best of intentions.

For Marian, please could you provide her with some green pantaloons to protect her modesty when she has to climb to her treehouse.

Her friend, Robin, is in dire need of a new pair of trousers as the ones he is currently wearing have several holes in very embarrassing places caused by having to hide in bramble bushes. The Sheriff's officers don't like leaving the main path, so Robin saves his ***skin*** in the prickly bush, but ***not*** his pants. Come to think of it, his skin gets a rough time of it as well, so perhaps some soothing balm might help.

John Little lost his stave in the river whilst defending his friends against the Sheriff's men. He is a big, strong man, perfectly capable of making a new stave but, unfortunately, he mislaid his axe and his dagger during the same contretemps. Could you perhaps send him a new tool kit?

Unusually, Will Scarlett has been engaging in fisticuffs. Strangely, he is much more of a dandy than a brawler. The poor man's hands are in a dreadful state, and I implore you to provide him with a manicure set and witch hazel to help repair his grazed knuckles.

The good Friar, who so very rigorously tends to the spiritual needs of his flock, hid his personal stock of beer and wine where no-one could find it. It would seem, however, that Much the Miller's son has been diverting the precious liquid for his Venison Bourguignon and Rabbit in Ale Gravy which everyone wolfs down with loud smacking of lips. But I digress. The friar would be beside himself with joy were he to receive a crate of claret from you.

Alan-a-dale has been bereft for many a week now. He no longer sings. This is having an effect on the morale of the rest of the group. I am told that he and Will were involved in a skirmish with Lord de Vere, one of the Sheriff's cousins, en route to Nottingham. During the fracas, de Vere was divested of twenty bags of silver pennies which were thrown onto a waiting cart. Sadly, they landed on top of Alan's lute which was crushed beyond musical recognition. I would suggest something like a drum but that would be too arduous for a wandering minstrel to carry around so I would plead with you to send him something to strum.

I send my thanks to you and hope that all wishes come true.

I remain
Yours very sincerely,

Lady Matilda Fitzwalter.

PS I have enclosed a map of the route from Worksop to Deninthewoods as John Little replaced all the signposts with silly pictures of the Sheriff.

Martin

by Hilary Lepine

Mervyn Crump felt acutely the burden of his name. He blamed his father for hanging on to it, his mother for marrying into it. How, thought Mervyn, looking round his studio - OK, garden shed - how could you possibly show or sell a painting signed *Mervyn Crump?*

Had the Mona Lisa been signed *Mervyn Crump,* he felt certain it would never have been noticed, let alone become probably the most famous painting in the world. Somehow, *'Crump's Mona Lisa'* didn't have the same ring as *'Leonardo's Mona Lisa'.* He wanted a powerful, dramatic name. Maybe just one syllable.

Mervyn breathed deeply on the intoxicating odour of oil paints, nutty aromatic linseed, the musty, woody smell of easel and bench, the earthy tang of canvas, the sharp acridity of turps in the jam jar that somehow always managed to sting the back of your nose. They were smells you carried around with you, penetrating your hair, your clothes.

His gaze travelled listlessly to his Mona Lisa, smiling, enigmatically he hoped, from the easel. In actual fact, it was his sister-in-law, the prettily named Marietta, though, wincing, he agonised over how she could willingly give up her maiden name of Marlowe to become a Crump when she married his brother.

For fifteen years, Mervyn had held a torch for Marietta, ever since his elder brother James had met her. It was a hopeless, unrequited passion of course, that saw him ensconced in his studio for hours at a time, refusing to allow anyone in, as he drew and painted his muse in various poses, some, in his youthful days, he admitted to himself with some shame, owing much to smuggled Page Threes of *The Sun*, since naturally he had never seen Marietta without clothes. Gradually, with growing maturity and artistic awareness, he had narrowed down his concept for the painting so that it would focus, like Leonardo's, on the countenance, and That Smile.

Marietta was indeed a beautiful woman, with the classic heart-shaped face - high cheekbones, wide set grey-green eyes, rosebud mouth. And she smiled a lot, in a way that lifted every heart that crossed her path. Desperately wanting to have her sit in his studio while he painted her from life, Mervyn could nevertheless never pluck up the courage to ask. He contented himself with photographs, of which there were many, for his parents, too, were in thrall to their lovely daughter-in-law. Marietta the Magnificent, his father called her. And meant it.

It had been Mervyn's intention to offer his goddess the painting on her birthday, which, portentously, he liked to think, was the same as his, 15th August, though six years later. It had never happened. The early works were stacked facing the walls, ashamed to show their faces, and the pile of aptly named and deeply unsatisfying Crumps was growing.

Mervyn had never bothered much with school, preferring instead to stare out of windows, watching clouds form, colours come and go, trees waving in breeze or gale. All he really wanted to do was to paint or draw. He'd never make a living doing that, cautioned his parents, teachers, and anyone else old enough to pontificate from the security of a job. He had to acknowledge it was true, but how was anyone called Mervyn Crump going to get a job anyway? The odds were stacked. You'd have to be super-cool to carry off a name like Mervyn, and he was far from that. And as for Crump – the sing-song bullying chant "Crumpit Dumpit" rang still as mercilessly in is ears as had his persecutors' chorus at school.

The job he eventually found was definitely a Mervyn job, he mused bitterly, grimly depositing milk bottles on doorsteps in the middle of the night. But it had the virtue of the hours – no one much to talk to him once he cleared the depot, and plenty of daylight left for painting after work. He could go back to the studio and try and capture That Smile. As Mervyn, frozen-fingered, tramped the endless paths of his round, he began to wonder - if a name matched a job, what would be a good name for a successful artist? Over twelve long years, many a cold night was passed in contemplation of a resounding artistic name. Sadly, Mervyn Crump did not have it in him to make the dramatic move to change his name.

Then came a blow. James had been offered a plum job with a company in the West Midlands. End of July, they were moving to Worcester. Marietta was leaving. Mervyn was devastated.

"You must come over as soon as we've settled," sang Marietta. "What about the weekend of our birthdays?"

***

"You have reached your destination," declared the sat nav. On the corner was Yew Tree Cottage, a story-book traditional country cottage. The painter in Mervyn was alerted. His eyes were drawn to the signpost opposite the cottage, pointing toward the improbably named village of Martin Hussingtree.

Martin Hussingtree. Mervyn was transfixed. That was it. The name to adopt. Martin - of Mars. The Warrior. The successful artist. Martin instantly felt strong, triumphant.

Sitting in the garden, under the apple tree, Marietta was a good subject. The rosebud lips just hinting at some mysterious, pleasurable thought, perhaps. The eyes watched Martin steadily as he worked. His muse, the goddess, liberating him from the shackles of Mervyn.

He returned to his studio with precious preliminary sketches. The smell was the same, but the energy was different. With sacred seriousness, Martin ceremoniously burnt every existing painting. Mervyn Crump was consigned to history. Martin Hussingtree took up his brushes.

With infinite care, Martin signed the finished, if belated, birthday gift. *Huss.* Marietta the Magnificent smiled back at him.

Dandelion

by Ivan Whomes

Seedling

“Oh, how lovely - a real little dandelion!”

Alice stood in the garden after her ninth birthday party wearing her green dress, waiting to say goodbye to the remaining guests. It was inevitable that Aunt Vera would home in on her. She was the jolly sort of aunt, and always put her face a bit too close to you when she was speaking. She even reached out and rubbed the girl's bright yellow braids between her fingers. Alice shuddered. She did not like being touched. Her mother came up and Alice was rescued, but not before several waiting children had noticed the imposition of the unwanted nickname.

Vegetative

Alice had never shaken it off - that name, that awful name. It had followed her from playground to classroom, from Primary to High School, and right through to Year Eight, even occasionally being used by a teacher. Thankfully it had been truncated to 'Dandy' (though to Alice still gross) or 'Danny' (slightly better). The braids had long gone and an insisted-on short haircut had replaced them.

Various attempts to reinstate her real name had failed, even amongst close friends. At home her parents called her Alice, but her obnoxious little brother was relentless in using her nickname, and when he was being a real pain he would chant the name time after time until she screamed at him to stop or stuck out a leg and kicked him.

Flowering

At Sixth Form College Alice specialized in art and design. Her hair was now dyed a raven black and hung down in lank witchy strands either side of her white face. Her eye shadow was purple, black and green. She had claimed the name 'Zero' for herself and insisted it be on all college lists and registers as well as on social media. She became renowned within the Art Department for her graphic novels full of apocalyptic visions, yelling faces, death and destruction.

Ripening

Her eclectic and colourful portfolio was growing and she was hopeful of a September place at the London College of Graphic Design if the exams came out all right. She needed a large central project however - a concept piece, bold, imaginative.

“I'm completely bloody stuck,” she said, spread-eagled on the lawn, or rather, the patch of grass out back of the college. The fashion for adopting dramatic new names had passed Tom by. He was simply known by everyone as 'Tom'. He and she had become an unlikely pairing. He was always reasonably conventionally dressed and seemed to be drifting in the direction of a career in electronics. The two of them had recently been involved together in a couple of drama productions, rather nihilistic plays, stark and despairing. She had acted and Tom had looked after the sound and lights, what there was of them; most of the action took place in sepulchral gloom. Tom could give his friend no positive advice on the direction of the exam project - he was far too laid back for that, but happily listened while she ruminated and pondered. He idly picked a few daisies and a fistful of greenery and threw them in a shower over her face.

"Bastard!" she shouted, laughing and levering herself up, brushing the foliage off her black tee shirt. As she did so, a yellow flower fell into her lap and her mind began to work.

She would need Tom to help her. The installation would be very large, five sections in all, and her meticulous plans involved wooden cut-out figures, strong struts to support them, many metres of wiring and boxes and boxes of small electric light bulbs. As the building costs grew, she went to her long-suffering parents for loans, sold some personal possessions and worked extra hours at the coffee shop. Tom's parents' garage was pressed into service as a workshop where cider and wine and regular deliveries of fast food accompanied the many hours of work put in by the pair.

They had discussed at great length whether to ask the college for permission, or to launch the piece without notice to anyone, in order to have a Banksy style guerrilla impact. In the end they approached one of their tutors who had a soft spot for conceptual work and received a positive response.

Two months after the birth of the project, the artist and Tom were ready.

In the early morning of the day of the exhibition of A level portfolios, a construction team assembled from the artist's close friends had been hidden behind tall screens as they worked, and a draped edifice ten metres high by thirty metres wide was ready for the start of the college day. Three hundred students, staff, parents and interested passers-by gathered before the formal start of the college day as, in silence, the artist, and Tom, stepped forward to grasp ropes which would pull aside the screens and covers.

The creation was revealed. Each of the five letters

was picked out in multi-coloured light. One after another they flashed on, until the whole word stood disclosed, a bright kaleidoscope of brilliance and shimmer against the prosaic concrete frontage of the college on that dull spring morning. The lights had been mounted on a green background; yellow flowers with a mixture of twisty art nouveau styled petals and bold stamen shapes had been painted within each letter, jostling with each other and spilling out beyond each letter's outlines.

And there were dandelions, hundreds of dandelions, strung together, within, around, all over the letters.

A L I C E

The name stood publicly proud as the diminutive figure of the black-clad artist walked up to, and took her place in front of, the third letter. She faced her audience and held out her arms wide.

"'I' am the middle of my name, its centre, its hub.

I have found myself.

I will be myself."

Alice held up a single dandelion and raised it to the sky.

Mary

by Hilary Lepine

The girl in the photograph smiled back. Reddish brown hair, masses of it, cascaded over her shoulders and down her back. "Titian" hair, her father had called it, somewhat obscurely she had thought, until she was about eight, when they had talked about the Italian painter Titian, and his famous paintings of women with that particular hue of red hair. Her favourite had been *Woman with a Mirror*, and for several years she had fantasised about being that woman, holding her long thick rope of hair, while a handsome stranger held a mirror for her to view both back and front. She never resolved who that stranger was, but she liked to retain the image of herself as remote and mysterious, and the hair became a signifier of that.

Mary found it now, the heavy mane pouring down her back. She collected it in her right hand and pulled it over her right shoulder. Not so vibrantly Titian these days, ever so slightly tinged with grey, it lay, shroud like, over her right breast. She smiled a small wry smile.

The oncologist had been practical, upbeat, matter of fact. He was optimistic that they could save the breast with a course of chemotherapy. Inevitably, she would lose her hair, that's the effect chemo has.

He had smoothly, courteously, dispassionately passed her on to the nurse, to the advice and support centre, to the Macmillan service, and thence here to the wig people.

With great respect and understanding, and with something akin to tenderness, they had gone through with Mary the stages she would encounter, the feelings that were likely to be aroused, over the loss of this, her crowning glory.

It was indeed her crowning glory, a statement of femininity, of allure, of wildness if she let it flow free; of poise and sophistication if she dressed it high on her head; and always of the remoteness and mystery she had conceived in her childhood fantasies. This head of hair always brought comment and attention, especially in her younger days, when it was so rich and remarkable in colour and vibrancy, whether from passers-by, admiring and envious friends, children in her class who wanted to plait it or brush it, or from lovers, who wanted to run their hands through it.

And now, it seemed, she was to lose it cruelly and arbitrarily. All of it. It would start to come out in clumps, within a couple of weeks of beginning chemotherapy. Oh, it would grow back - in about a year. People only usually need a wig for about a year. Of course, it may grow back differently. Curly.

She was advised to cut it short now, so that the wig would fit better. She would not get a wig over all that hair anyway, even while it was falling out. So she had to commit to self-mutilation - cut off her hair.

She had done that once, when she was around eleven, to the horror of her family and the amusement and awe of her friends. Her mother had actually cried after Mary, sick of the school rule on plaits had hacked off one.

There had been a moment of suspended disbelief as she looked at the beautiful, amputated plait lying on the kitchen worktop, cut-off, rejected, and already somehow losing its lustre. Her grief and remorse had known no bounds, compounded when her parents discovered "the act", as her father pontifically called it, and amplified even further when the other plait had to come off, and she ended up with a bob. The bob made her feel tomboyish, elfin, practical, and she felt she could be naughty, but never arch, as she visualised herself in her romantic daydreams.

It had taken about eighteen months to get her hair back anywhere like it had been. She had resolved never to have it cut again. She remembered now, with wry amusement, how she had written childish poems *in memoriam,* comparing her loss of remoteness, mystery and feminine allure to Samson's loss of strength after Delilah cut his hair.

So now she had to break that vow and cut her hair. Take the scissors, and again mutilate herself. Then go around for the next year or so, wearing a skull cap - to soak up the sweat, they said, wigs make your head sweat more - with this wig thing on top. She had tried on several, all a pretty good colour match, but somehow, though the hair fell long and luxurious, it did not quite meet the mark. And it was synthetic. You had to take off the wig and wash it - "swish it around" - in a basin. They didn't recommend natural hair, more difficult to maintain, and very expensive, especially if you were only likely to need it for a year or so.

What would she look like with no hair? It changed the shape of one's head, revealed bone structure, changed the balance of ears, eyes, and eyebrows. Why was it that a man could shave his head and acquire gravitas, sex appeal, distinction, whereas women who did the same could be considered lesbian, aggressive, challenging, shocking, *unfeminine*? It was just hair.

But it's not just hair, she reasoned. It's a prize, a commodity, second only in the femininity stakes to breasts. A woman without hair is hardly a woman at all. Without the hair, who would she be? She could no longer be remote and mysterious; she would suddenly be up-front and in-your-face to all those who looked upon her - as indeed they would.

A parade of shaven-headed women passed before her. She had to admit they did look sexy, dramatic. Interesting and *alive*. You had to have courage, a strong sense of self. People might come up and envy your scalp, and wish they had the nerve to do it.

Mary looked in the mirror, trying to visualise her skull, shaven.
"What would you have me know?" she asked her reflection.
"You are beautiful, any way you are. Your hair is not you. You are not your hair. You don't have to give a shit. Why pretend? Get some glam eye make-up, shave the bugger off! Go out and celebrate!"

She picked up the phone and dialled her hairdresser.

Seat 41

by Claire Walker

Welcome aboard this delayed 12:42 service to Norwich. We wish to inform passengers that the champagne and oyster trolley is not available today. We will be calling at...

Manchester Piccadilly to Chesterfield

Rob

The train is already packed, but that's okay because - unbelievable - there is a seat. An actual *seat*. Bag hefted onto the shelf with a fleeting concern for the wedding suit inside then plonk down with *FourFourTwo* and a packet of prawn cocktail crisps. This is a rubbish seat, no window to speak of but the view's boring anyway, and it's better than standing by the toilet like a pillock. There was no getting out of this, but the wedding's going to be hell, when the girl you love is getting married to your best mate. It's been hell for the past ten years. Down the pub of a Sunday or at the game, there's always been this bitter need to hit something, preferably Jimmy, but that's not fair. He doesn't know, and he can't help loving Alice. Who wouldn't be in love with Alice, with her fiery hair and pale skin that looks like it might taste of cream if you licked it? And why wouldn't Alice choose Jimmy, who's a gas fitter *and* has a degree in economics, over a labourer who didn't even turn up for his GCSEs? Katie at work says uni's not everything and some girls like a bloke who's good with his hands. Katie's alright. She nearly got asked if she wanted to be a plus-one, but any aggro at the wedding would put her right off. She's not Alice, but pretty enough and good for a laugh. Alice...Alice hasn't been around for weeks, what with all the wedding faff, and now the thought of her brings on that itch under the scab of hurt and - weird - it *is* a scab, not an open festering wound any more. What's that all about? Still, no point moping about it now, time enough for that later. Now there's just crisps and football. To be honest, what else does a bloke need?

Chesterfield to Alfreton

Susan

What's this? A crisp packet. Really, some people. A brisk dusting of the seat before sitting down. A journey of just eleven minutes, and yet such an expanse of Arctic tundra to cross. The call came yesterday afternoon, when the washing up was nearly finished. Rushing to answer it, and hearing Tracy's voice. *It's about Alan*...So odd, calling one's father by his Christian name. Such a lack of respect.

But then Alan never deserved respect. Turned out he had cancer. Sometimes it seemed like everyone you knew had cancer, but it had never come this close to home before. But how could you call it close when you haven't seen your brother for forty-odd years? Listening in growing consternation, suds dripping onto the carpet. Sitting there for ages afterwards, stunned. Unbidden, the awful memory of Alan's insolence, of Dad turning to yell a retort then the impact and the reek of petrol and the acrid taste of burning at the back of the throat. Both parents lifeless in the front, Alan scrambling across the back seat. The pain...Alan just standing there on the verge and staring, immobile, while your parents' lives ebbed away and yours hung in the balance, until someone else came and took you away. The hatred has gone - all that hate had been *so* exhausting - and so has the worst of the pain. Forgiveness is going too far, but some kind of rapprochement might have been in order before now. The time had never been right, though. A tiny, malevolent voice, somewhere deep inside, one instantly, ruthlessly quashed, whispers that the cancer is just payment for what he did. But fifty-seven, with only weeks left to live - no one deserves that. Bile wells, hot and bitter, and there's a stab of pain close to the heart. Surely that isn't...*guilt*? And definitely not grief, not for him. No. The train is slowing. Gather up bag, flowers - appropriate, or not? - and move down the aisle to the doors.

Grantham to Norwich

Zoe

There's a flower on the seat - tiny, pink, and crushed. A quick flick sends it to the floor. This seat faces backwards but that's okay, it's good to watch places disappear into the distance, or it would be if there was a windowx. The ticket to Norwich cost a bomb and I don't know where the place is, but it can't be any worse than Grantham, than the Home. Leaving that crappy dump was the best idea ever. And none of the - air quotes - "residential support workers" will notice, or even care. Not even Alison, who's not bad really but everyone reckons she's a lezzer cos she always wears dungarees. Mackenzie won't care and that's actually fine cos he's a prat and a crap boyfriend. The police came for him yesterday, he got caught on camera nicking chocolate. Someone said what's the big deal and Alison said it's a big deal cos it starts with Mars bars and ends with him torching the dogs' home or something, like that kid up north did last year. In the bag is a wad of cash, nicked from the office when someone was stupid enough to leave it lying about, biscuits and apples and a bottle of Coke and Ziggy, the teddy Mum left. He still smells a bit like hospitals, but that was years ago and he should get chucked out now. Not today though. God, here comes that pukey feeling again. It's been happening a lot lately, don't know why, but it'll go away. Wonder what Norwich will be like? Whatever, there'll be jobs and how hard can it be to get one? In a nursery, or something, that'd be good. Yeah, everything is going to work out fine.

We are now approaching Norwich, where this train terminates. We wish all passengers a safe and pleasant onward journey.

Bus Home

by Ivan Whomes

His heart had started thumping already and the bus wasn't due at the village stop for fifteen minutes. But he didn't care. For he was embarking on his most exciting journey ever.

It was a real disadvantage living three miles from the town. For instance, he always needed to catch the bus home from Newtown High, which left no time for mixing with the others, swapping news, chatting with the girls; and this term he especially missed these opportunities. Josie was in his class. She was popular, mostly with noisy laughing groups of girls, but had her studious side. She smiled a lot; occasionally, he thought, at him. There was a sort of willowy, fluid way she presented herself, and she always dressed stylishly, as far as the uniform rules would allow. Miniskirts were now firmly in fashion and she wore hers with confidence, flair even. The way she cut her hair was similar to Sandie Shaw.

He had confessed his yearning to Barry, who had encouraged him to do something about it.

“No point in just making those sheep's eyes at her and putting on that goofy grin - go and speak to her - ask her out.”

A couple of weeks later a group of students from the local university had visited their class to advertise a drama session to be held the next Friday afternoon. They would be performing extracts from plays, and some improvisation. On asking for a show of hands from those pupils who would like to come, the response came hesitantly at first, but soon hands started going up - maybe twelve or fifteen, mostly girls - and one was Josie!

Did he dare? Richard and Joe, two friends of his, had volunteered and he felt the courage to join them. I've done it! he thought. It's like a declaration of love...almost!

He pushed open the door with a mixture of excitement and apprehension. The room had the cabbagey, sweaty smell of recently vacated school hall, the sound of echoing chatter and scuff of school shoes on wooden floor. He cast a discreet look at the girls and, yes, Josie was there, tie loosened and blazer discarded.

“Please pair off for our next exercise,” said Linda, the student who was leading the session. “Boy and girl would be nice, but I think we'll soon run out so two girls will be fine,” she laughed. “You are close friends or girl and boyfriend, and you have had a quarrel and need to make up. So, two minutes to discuss together with your partner then we'll see what you've come up with."

Did he have the nerve? Would it really happen? Yes! Josie fixed him with an enquiring sort of smile. "Shall we?"
He caught a sharp, floral scent as she sidled up to him.
"Yes, that'd be fab!"

He was too nervous to relax into the improvisation, and he knew his was a stilted performance. But as the group broke up he found himself saying, "Perhaps we can meet up sometime - would you like to go to the pictures?"

"Yes, let's!" she had replied.
"*The Graduate*'s' on at the Essoldo - shall we meet outside tomorrow at seven-thirty?" he said, guessing that that might be the right time.

"Okay, see you there," and she whirled off with her friends, giving him a wave over her shoulder. He would have a very long wait for the next bus home, but he didn't mind - he was already basking in a glorious glow of contentment. She had said yes!

And that's why he was standing at the village bus stop on that drizzly Saturday evening. Barry had said, "Don't wear any part of your school uniform, for God's sake - it's an X film!" so he'd put his best suit on. He carried a polythene bag with a box of chocolates in it which he dangled self-consciously from his fingers. Suddenly the bus pulled up, spraying dirty water all over his newly cleaned shoes. He jumped up on the platform into the garishly lit interior. It was dark outside and he could see little through the rain-spotted windows, but soon he glimpsed the town centre lights, the police station, the town hall, the Marks and Spencer.

He stood out of the rain at the entrance to the cinema. He was early for his date. Soon people started arriving - nearly all of them couples, hand in hand or arm in arm, trotting swiftly up the three steps to the foyer, to be enclosed in the wrap-around comfort of the Essoldo, dry and warm and cosy.

He affected some interest in the glossy posters of forthcoming attractions, but always with one eye on the High Street. The lights of passing cars and buses made yellow streaks on the wet roads. Then the figure of a young girl came scuttling through the rain toward him, head down under a bright orange umbrella. She removed a headscarf and shook her dark hair free. She was wearing a short, light blue coat and white knee boots. She glanced up. It wasn't Josie. The girl looked past him and waved to a friend. The two girls linked arms and bounced happily into the foyer.

He looked around him. There were fewer customers coming up the steps now and soon the trickle dried up altogether. A few minutes later a uniformed commissionaire emerged and took in the advertising placard.

“Main feature's started, sir.”
“Yes, thank you.”

He looked at his watch. Seven-fifty. Soon he would be trudging through the rain back to the bus station. Because he knew now.

She wasn't coming.

Undercurrent

by Ivan Whomes

The channel had narrowed, making rowing impossible; the bulbous tubers protruding from the riverbank and the lianas hanging from the bordering trees rubbed and caressed the small boat's gunwales. The smell given off by the green slime almost made him gag. He shipped the oars and discovered a paddle which he thought would help to guide the vessel forward. The boat, however, needed no extra propulsion - there seemed to be a strong current pulling it silently forward.

The trees crowded in on the channel, causing a shadowy gloom to descend. A large tuber struck a rowlock and exploded a dark purple liquid on his hand. He quickly scrubbed the glutinous deposit off using his handkerchief, but the sickly odour was indescribable.

The folk at the retreat had been very kind. Iter House was quiet and calm with large airy rooms. Enablers and facilitators had provided opportunities for meditation, therapy and gentle exercise. He had noticed that occasionally a resident would be handed a small card bearing the three words:

TIME TO GO

He could not, now, remember large parts of his previous life, the guilt, the regret, nor why exactly he had enrolled. But he had recently experienced an overpowering sensation that he should no longer be here.

There were no locked doors at Iter, no monitoring technology, no supervisors. Three times he had attempted to walk back the way he had come. But three times twisting paths and inescapable maze-like alleys of green had returned him to the isolated mansion.

One night when darkness had fallen and become complete, he had dressed, left the house and followed a previously unnoticed path twisting through an uncultivated wildness. He passed redundant ivy-covered sheds and derelict outbuildings. And then he was knee deep in marsh at the source of the river. Downstream, partly hidden behind a veil of vegetation, he had set eyes on the boat.

Rotting, narrow but apparently reasonably watertight, he had bailed it out with cupped hands, pushed it from the reeds and installed himself upon its wet, green seat. Back in his room, propped against a lamp, remained a white card.

TIME TO GO

How long had he been travelling? Time had ceased to be measurable. The sun hadn't risen; neither had it set. It was perpetual dusk. In the complete absence of birdsong, the only sounds were the quietly insistent slap of water on the prow and the sibilant whisper of bloated foliage sliding over the vessel's timbers.

He had been perching on his wooden, backless seat for hours, days, weeks...

He felt no hunger, no thirst...

The river began to broaden out. Rotten leaves no longer covered its surface. Fingers of ill-shaped vegetation withdrew their forays into the boat. Long wispy fronds ceased to stroke his face.

The jungle had disappeared behind him, and his boat was drifting on a clear lake. There were signs of cultivation on the banks; fields of crops - yellow, caramel, umber - starting to sway in the breeze. He stretched out his arms to grasp the oars ready to row for the shore but his hands couldn't get a grip and the oars slid through his fingers into the lake, submerging themselves quietly beneath the surface.

The sound of running water, like the babble of a hundred children, now intruded on the silence. The boat started to spin in slow circles, the hands of a clock turned by an implacable key. A giant cloud of spray appeared at the lake's perimeter to which it was now being drawn, steadily and gracefully. His fingers ineffectually attempted to clutch at the wooden seat as the speed increased. The roar of the water hammered his ears. Then the flimsy craft balanced on the brink for a long, long second before joining the waterfall on its headlong plunge to the rocks below.

TIME TO GO

Ink

by Di Bettinson

Matty Harris was very proud of his tattoos. His children knew this all too well. He had told them the stories behind each picture, many a time. He always said he would allow himself to have just a few. Well, let's face it, they hurt, and he didn't do pain. Matty didn't like pain of any sort and the thought of covering his skin with ink was too much to bear. He was full of admiration for those who battled that agony to cover their bodies with colour. But despite the discomfort, he decided long ago that some memories warranted more than a photograph. Each one of his pictures had its own tale. He would always be pleased to tell, and as time went on, elaborate on their history to anyone who asked.

On his right upper arm, he had a picture of a surfboard with '1st' written on it. One could possibly think he had won a surfing competition, but truth be told it was to celebrate his first ever surf lesson, when visiting Hawaii. He wasn't very good at it and ended up being rescued by a lifeguard. He had to pay extra for losing the board as well. But the memory of just being there was enough.

There was a picture of a snail sitting on a frog. So, how else do you denote the wonderful food he devoured in France. He had been dared to try snails in garlic sauce followed by battered and deep-fried frog's legs. The taste he could never replicate but, oh, so delicious. Of his food pictures he also had an ice cream for Italy, beef tomato for Spain, a burger for America, and for home? His favourite fish and chips.

Some of the tattoos were obvious and didn't need any explanation. The kangaroo was of course from his first visit to Australia. The sunflower for Ukraine. Pyramid? Needless to say, Egypt.

Matty's gap year, when he finished university, had turned into a five-year mission to see as much of the world as he could. He was proud to say he had been to Everest. Base camp that is, as altitude sickness prevented him from going further. But of course, he had a great picture of the North Face, no less, on one shoulder.

The image of Machu Picchu required a large amount of ink and several visits to the tattoo studio. And that one really hurt. But he had been there, so it had to be done. Then of course there was the depiction of the Taj Mahal, the Hanging Gardens of Babylon, the Grand Canyon and of course the Great Barrier Reef, that was a hard one. The Great Wall of China snaked its way around his arm.

So, in fact, Matty was rather full of ink.

After all his gallivanting around the globe he had a yearning to come home and perhaps even settle. Find a career and earn some real money. Up until now he had only needed to earn enough to get him to the next place. The next tattoo shop. The next Ink Artist, each of whom had their own skills and interpretations.

Margret Harris was so excited to see her son, but even though she had been warned she was shocked to see him *bathed in colour* as he called it. She was of the generation that viewed tattoos as big blue bruise-like smudges on the arms of old men. She looked down on them and considered them as a predilection of drunken sailors.

To see her perfect son so defiled was a great sadness to her. Another shock in store for Margaret was the fact that Matty had not been travelling alone. She did not realise that Jazz had been with him the whole time. Although she knew Jazmine from Matty's university days, nothing in his rare communications home had mentioned the fact that she was with him. Still less the fact that they had married in the Elvis Chapel in Las Vegas. He even had a tattoo of that. Well of course he did, thought Margaret. Sadness enveloped her again because she would never be able to attend his wedding.
As time elapsed Matty and Jazz settled, their

wandering days over. Apart from the odd week in Ibiza, and when the children came along, they invited Margaret to accompany them. The children grew and neither Samuel nor Emily showed any signs of wanting to adorn their bodies with pictures like their father. He naturally had tattoos of them as babies. After all, their arrivals were two of the most important events of his life.

There was one piece of ink that Matty could not explain. It had just appeared one time when he and Jazz had got very drunk on Aguardiente, a brandy type drink made from sugar cane in Colombia. He had been ill for a few days after that binge and swore he was never going to drink again. Although he said he wanted to forget all about that horrible experience, Jazz had other ideas.

While he was still not quite himself, she had a tattoo artist write some words in Colombian in a circle around his belly button. This had an arrow pointing up toward his chest. Many years later she told him what the words said.

'In case of emergency, this way up.' They still laugh about it.

There was a space in the centre of Matty's chest and that was where he had his very last tattoo. There was just room for a small picture, taken from a photo that had travelled around the world with him.

And the words RIP Mum 12/12/2020.

Off World

by Di Bettinson

Rob Taylor noted the car travelling ahead of him. His neighbour Caris in her little sports car. Knowing she had been heading for the garden centre that morning, he suspected she had a boot full of compost. He also knew he would be asked to carry it into the back garden for her. Well, that's what neighbours are for after all. At least he would get a nice cup of coffee and a piece of cake for his efforts.

The Interstellar Corporation Vessel Champion was too late to save the ship of the planet Scient from its untimely destruction.
Among the debris was an unexpected piece of ancient technology.
"It is a car, Captain," the first officer said.
"A car?"
"A four wheeled vehicle prevalent on earth up until the late twentieth century."
"I do know what a car is, thank you, Mr Swain."
"Two occupants, both showing vital signs of life, Sir, but in a state of suspension," Mr Swain said.
"Well, we had better bring it on board, and take the occupants to sick bay. I need to talk to someone on Scient and inform them of the fate of their ship."

In a meeting with the ship's doctor, first officer, one of the ship's counsellors and an historian, Captain

Moore asked, “What have we got then, people? Doctor, the occupants are alive and well?”
“Indeed, Captain, a woman in her mid-thirties and a teenage girl. By the looks of them mother and daughter. Still in suspension at present.”
“Mr Jonas, the car, what can you tell us?”
“The car was manufactured in the year 2014, a Mazda MX5. On examination of the clothing of the occupants, I would put the actual year to be 2016. In the storage compartment there are several plastic bags of material used for the growing of plants. Compost. Also, there are several bags containing foodstuff that was popular at the time,” the historian told them.
“Still using plastic at that time?”
“Single use plastic in fact.”
“Can we store that, without deterioration?”
“Perfectly. After all, plastic has been found in perfect condition many centuries after manufacture.”
“I have spoken to the leading minister of Scient. He told me that the lifting of the vehicle was an unfortunate error, and they do not yet have the technology to return it to the correct time and placing. They are working on it, but it will be a few years from now before they can rely on it,” Captain Moore said.
“We can’t keep those women in suspension for much longer Captain. They will soon show signs of tissue breakdown,” the doctor said.

"Which bring us to at least one other problem. If they are to stay with us until the Scients can perfect their replacement technology, not only will they be frightened but we will have to erase the memory of them being here."
"Our own scientists are working on something similar, to help those suffering post traumatic symptoms, we may be able to use that. Depending on how long they are with us," counsellor Elish said.
"Right, prepare quarters for them and wake them up. We will have a lot of explaining to do and you will be busy, Counsellor."

Caris Spender woke up in a comfortable bed but in a room she did not recognise. Glancing to her right she saw her daughter Evelyn sleeping peacefully. A woman was sitting in a chair close by.
"Don't be afraid Caris, you are safe," she said. "My name is Elish."
"How do you know my name, who are you, and where in hell's name are we?"
"Mum. What's happened?" Evelyn asked, woken by the sound of her mother's voice.
"I don't know, love, I really don't."
"This will come as a shock to you, but I can show you where you are." Elish turned and looked at a wall, a panel slid back to reveal the vista of a black sky with pin pricks of light.
"What is this? Some sort of cinema screen? It's like something out of a Sci-fi film," Caris said.

"No, that is what people on earth call outer space. The year as counted on Earth is 4021."
"Mum?"
Elish explained the situation and then took them on a tour of the spaceship. It was to Caris and Evelyn like a small town, with schools, places of worship, shops, in fact everything a body could need for a prolonged journey.

Caris and Evelyn had moved and settled many times in their lives, being the family of a serving soldier, but never so far, nor with such strange people. As the years went by, they stopped asking when they could go home. Evelyn attended school. Caris found satisfying work in the on-board museum, where her car was the prime exhibit. Life went on and after their initial fear and sadness they lived quite happily. They spoke with Elish often and were always reassured that they would go back to her life at the exact point that her car was lifted from Earth.

One day Captain Moore came to visit.
"The Scients tell me they have perfected their replacement procedures, so, we need to prepare you for your return to your own lives," he told them.
"How can we do that knowing all this?" Caris asked.
"That is something else we need to do, erase your memories of being here."
"What? Do we have to?" Evelyn said.
"Yes, I'm afraid so. You cannot go back to your time

with the knowledge you have gained by being here. So, prepare we must."

Rob Taylor glanced in his rear-view mirror and noted the car travelling behind him. His neighbour Caris in her little sports car. Knowing she had been heading for the garden centre that morning, he suspected she had a boot full of compost. He also knew he would be asked to carry it into the back garden for her. Well, that's what neighbours are for after all. At least he would get a nice cup of coffee and a piece of cake for his efforts.

Landscapes, Seascapes and Crocodile Rock

by Midge Mellor

He had known for weeks that his chances of being able to stay were next to nothing. His father was a self-opinionated, narrow-minded tyrant who had tormented his mother for years. In his world, men ruled the house and women did their bidding. Boys were schooled to be leaders and girls...well, girls were a waste of space, good enough to cook and clean but not much else.

The fact that Jack had grown up with poetry in his head and painting in his fingers incensed his father who tried to thrash the Arts out of him and instil masculine qualities his father thought so necessary to get on in the world. As soon as Jack was twelve, his father had enrolled him into the Army Cadets 'to give him some backbone'. On his first training trip to

Millport, Jack learned new skills like digging a latrine, making a hide from branches and bracken and how to keep warm on cold autumn nights. He volunteered himself as assistant cook making Scotch pancakes and thick soups. Secrets passed down from mum to son so he would never need to be hungry. And, in the quiet of the night, he sketched likenesses of the Corporal and the Captain, which the other cadets used as target practice using stones and bits of burnt sausage.

Jack had always been a neat and well-ordered child. A mother's dream; his mother's dream. Jack had tried to shield her from his father's rages. But the years of mental abuse had taken their toll and after months of the deepest depression, she lay down in the river that led to the Firth of Clyde and let the water take her life.

His father cried no tears but set about arranging his own life to ensure there was someone to take care of his every need. Aunt Ellen came to stay for a month and her fussing and bustling suited her brother very well. He would look to secure something rather more permanent once his exploited sister went back to her family. He would pack his son off to a cousin in Leicestershire and live the high life.

Jack's emotions took diverse and conflicting

directions. Hate spilled out from his heart. Vengeance was in danger of dominating his thinking. Sadness streamed from his eyes. But it was self-preservation that prevailed. He began to store away what he would need. He allowed himself just enough to fit into a backpack and gathered together the essentials: toiletries, pan, spoon, knife, water bottle, enamel mug, sleeping bag, camping gas cooker, waterproof cape, three T shirts, two pairs of jeans, spare pair of trainers stuffed with socks and underwear. He searched out his micro-fibre towels and a pack of space blankets, courtesy of the Army cadets. He scoured the shed for a trowel and unearthed a washing line which he knew would come in handy. Neat folding and careful packing ensured he had room for his artist's pads, paints and pencils, a roll of plastic bags, cycle repair kit, a torch and batteries. The backbone-building pop up tent slotted into the back of the backpack.

He watched Aunt Ellen, up to the elbows in flour and yeast, pummelling the dough. She would be too absorbed in her bread making to be interested in what Jack was doing. He slipped into the cellar with the backpack, checked his bike and, satisfied that everything was in good working order, made his way back upstairs. Aunt Ellen had moved onto peeling vegetables for the beef casserole she was making for dinner tonight. A pity he wouldn't be there to enjoy it. Jack sighed, but he had one last task. Taped to the underside of the drawer in his father's desk was an envelope packed with five-pound notes. His mother had shown it to him months ago, saying it was her escape fund. Perhaps if she had used it, she would still be alive, he thought miserably. But now it was part of *his* escape kit, Shoving the money into his pocket and putting on his jumper and parka, he returned downstairs, collected backpack and bike and left by the cellar door to make his first leap of faith.

Cycling down to Largs terminal, he made it just in time to get the nine forty-five ferry to Cumbrae and stepped off the boat eleven minutes later at the Slip. The beauty of this small island made him want to forget everything else and just sit and draw. The curve of the shoreline, the hills of Arran on the horizon, the sands stretching out - they all invited him to sit and capture the serenity of this pocket-sized piece of heaven. And sit down he did, pulling out his pad and pencil to sketch, not the cadet officers this time but the soft waves gently spraying the golden grains of sand and the Crocodile Rock.

Self-preservation kicked in several hours later and Jack reluctantly stowed away his drawings and tuned his mind to the must haves before the day was through. He cycled to the grocers and bought some staple items to keep body and soul together. That took ten pounds from his precious reserves, and he quickly decided he would have to live on porridge, soup and scotch pancakes for as long as he could.

Jack cycled along the coastline until he saw a holiday park offering accommodation for far more than he could afford. But just behind it, at the top of a gently sloping hill, was a spinney in a clearing. A godsend! Those bushes and small trees would offer him shelter and he jubilantly made his way up to his new home.

Life on Cumbrae was so good for Jack. He blended in well as a permanent feature amongst the visitors who came and went. His tent kept out the rain and his camping stove served up one pot meals, mugs of tea and the much-appreciated pancakes. The holiday park staff didn't seem to notice the healthy looking young man who popped twenty pence into the coin operated shower every morning and was rewarded with hot water and a sneaky chance to wash himself and his clothes. The washing line, tied between two bushes, helped the drying process and careful folding meant the lack of an iron did not ruin the look of his outfits. On rainy days, the waterproof cape provided cover for the washing line and the tea shop had a helpful radiator. The staff there refilled his water bottle every day and offered him hot coffee in return for wittily drawn sketches of the manager. On hot days, he washed his coat and prayed for fine weather until it was completely dry again.

The summer passed and Jack braved the dark evenings and cold nights of winter. His escape fund would last until March as long as he remained frugal. The gas canisters were his greatest expense but he had vowed never to light a camp fire because of damage to the small woodland. The holiday park remained open throughout the year advertising Halloween, and Bonfire Night, Christmas Breaks and Hogmanay celebrations. Thank God for coin operated showers. When loneliness and sadness threatened, he wrote poems about the fishermen and the magnificence of the Cathedral of the Isles. He painted the hills of Arran seen in the distance. He drank hot water and ate porridge and slept in a space blanket, inside his sleeping bag. It was hard for a fifteen-year-old but he pushed through it, remembering the suffering his mother had endured. Her distress made him all the more determined to live a happy life.

Spring brought more tender temperatures to the island. The stack of drawings and paintings he worked on throughout the winter would prove to be the turning point as Jack used the last of his money to rent a stall at the Wednesday market on the harbour. The visitors to the island enthused over the ethereal images of boats and rocky shorelines. They looked at the poems written in italics on an outline of Cumbrae and found them inspiring. By three o'clock he had sold everything. He cycled back to his tent by way of the grocers and made a celebratory batch of pancakes.

The following year, as well as growing his folio of paintings, he harvested tomatoes, grown from seed in a plastic bucket he had found next to the harbour wall. And maybe his version of Pasta al Pomodoro had only three ingredients – cheap spaghetti, water and home-grown Roma tomatoes. But Jack didn't care. Who needed chillies, garlic, basil and cheese? Life was improving by the minute.

By the time he was eighteen, his reputation had spread amongst the island population who regarded him as a rare talent and free-spirited artist who painted landscapes for the hoteliers, pictures of the Crocodile Rock for the visitors and small seascapes for the harbour cafes. The craft shop owners offered to print his poems on hand made paper and sell them for him. He was making money and changes would soon follow.

When his tent in the spinney became a tourist attraction, Jack knew he would have to leave. Three years of tent life, still with one knife, one pan and one spoon, had helped him to become a self-reliant, confident person who could withstand difficulties and come through hardship. But he hated the persistent invasion of visitors into the small woodland and the assumption that he wouldn't mind being asked to draw a pencil sketch of Freddie or Laura or Willow the spaniel.

The most alarming thought thudded its way through his head. During those three years he had only needed to replace his underwear and a T shirt that had ripped on the gorse bush. Now it was time to replace his home. And that opened the floodgates of legal adulthood. A national Insurance number, council tax, the revenue people, gas and electricity - oh my god it was daunting. He had no fear of anything on his island but official paperwork was terrifying. He had survived without technology. He had led the simple life and now it was all becoming so complicated.

It was Morag who came up with the idea.

"There's a studio flat above our craft shop. It's filthy dirty and the plaster has come off the walls. To be honest, it is a pig sty, but if you are willing to do the renovations, you can have it rent free for six months. What d'you say? And I'll give you a hand with your paperwork."

It was a difficult decision for Jack to make. By his third pancake he had a list of goods and bads. For a start, he knew nothing about plastering and hadn't a clue how much it would cost to pay someone to do it. On the good side, he knew he would eventually paint mural mountains and the green, orange and bronze of his spinney on the walls. He would have to find furniture - what would it be like to sleep in a bed after three years of a sleeping bag?

He had just under three thousand pounds from the sale of his artwork. Would that be enough to cover everything? When he left home three years ago he had exactly three *hundred* pounds. With that sobering thought in his head, he knew he would make the second leap of faith and say yes to Morag's idea.

The next three years were a mixture of hard worked-for successes and glorious failures - the plaster fell off the walls twice. The paintings flowed out from him. The plaster finally stayed on the walls, the pig sty transformed into a bijou studio which took on the most delicate, dappled woodland shades.

Serendipity also played her part by bringing to the craft shop a mainland visitor who bought one of Jack's paintings and several of his poems printed on the cream handmade paper. The visitor had ideas for building up the Glasgow Gallery's gift shop and she wanted to give display space to the works of Scotland's up and coming young artists. With Jack's work she instinctively knew she was onto a winner.

It took eighteen months of meetings on the island and reams of correspondence before the gallery management finally persuaded Jack to come back to the mainland for the opening of his first exhibition.

He agreed only after Morag promised that she would come as well. They stayed for twenty-four hours, drank a little champagne and managed to get the last ferry from Largs to the Cumbrae Slipway on a rainy Sunday evening. Jack and his island were as one again.

The critics called him a modern-day Turner but to the islanders he remained a free-spirited artist who painted landscapes for the hoteliers, pictures of Crocodile Rock for the visitors and small seascapes for the harbour cafes.

Trailer Adventures

by Di Bettinson

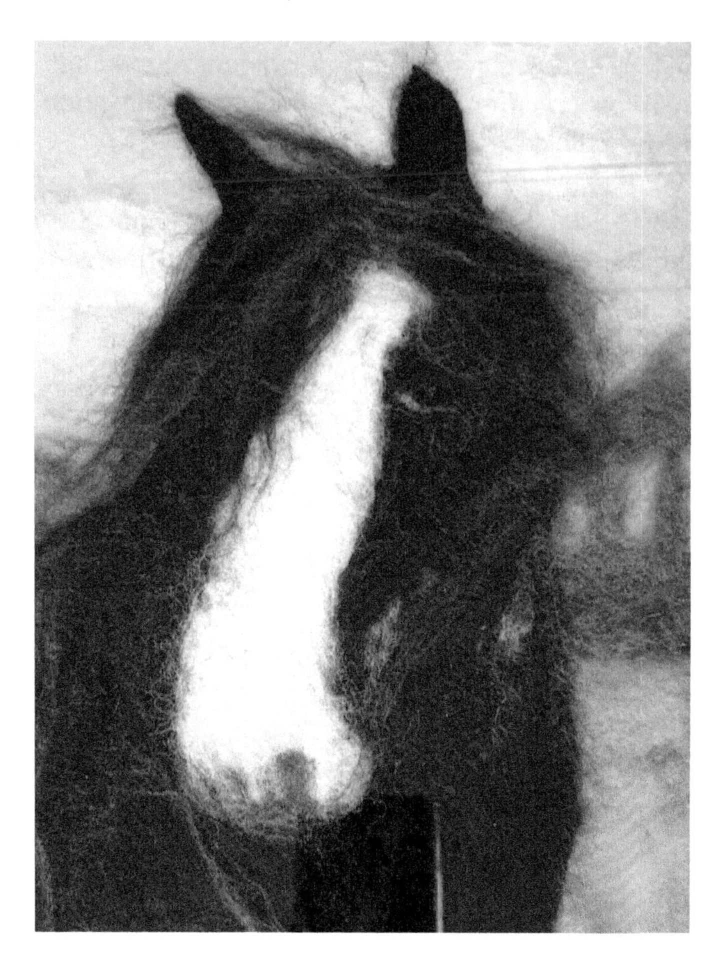

The horse trailer has been backed up the yard and the tail ramp put down. Well, if she thinks I'm getting in there she has another think coming.

She, being my twarm. The humans that look after horses are known to us as twarms because instead of four legs they have two arms. Very useful for making sure we get the correct amount of feed and cleaning up after us. Servants really, some good some, well least said about them the better.

She does look rather smartly dressed in a white shirt and her pale cream jodhpurs. I wonder where she thinks we are going? She has spent several hours grooming me until my coat shines and my mane and tail are knot free. She even washed my feathers. The saddle and bridle have already been stowed in the pickup. She's climbing into overalls, she definitely wants to keep clean. Maybe I can do something about that as well, but the overalls only leave her head and face for me to slobber on.

There is one thing she has forgotten though, my breakfast, it's still outside the stable. Ah, she has remembered, she is coming over for it. But wait, she's putting it in the bloody trailer. Well maybe I will go in this time just to lull her into a false sense of security.
So, with head collar and travel boots on, which make me walk as if my legs are made of jelly, I comply and decide to walk straight on the trailer to get my breakfast. She has even tied a hay net up for me to eat on the journey. Very efficient.

All tied in and all doors shut off we go. It's only about quarter of a hay net away, so not too far.

I don't really mind going out like this. I get to see some friends and all I have to do is prance around a ring for a few minutes. Walking, trotting, extended trot and a little bit of canter, sometimes they ask for a gallop. Then stand still so some bossy person in the middle can have a good look at us. The grass in the ring is usually good stuff but I'm never allowed to eat any until after I've done my bit of showing off. This time the bossy person is coming towards me with a small flappy thing. I'm not entirely sure about it but my twarm seems really pleased and so I let the bossy one tie it to my bridle. A red rosette.

After more chats with friends, hers and mine, and plenty of grass eating, it would seem to be time to go home. After all it is getting quite dark.

No, this time I am not getting in the trailer. There is only a hay net to temp me, and I like the grass here. I am standing with two feet on the ramp, but I don't think I'll move any further forward. Well let's face it she weighs a lot less than me so if I don't want to go, she can't make me. I am over five hundred kilos and can stand my ground.

She leads me around again hoping I will walk on, but I dodge to the side. Around we go so I dodge the other way.

Next comes the pressure, release method. She pulls hard and if I make the slightest move forward, she stops pulling. I know all about it and just pull back.

Some of her friends come behind me with a long line around my rump trying to guide me in. I just sit on that. Then decide to go into full rearing mode with a few bucks and squeals, for good measure. Some other busybodies came over and tell my twarm "That horse is frightened. You should do some desensitizing."

"Well, when we finally get home, I may well do that, again," she tells them, knowing that I am not scared, I just like to put my point across. And today I decide not to go on the journey home. This grass is much nicer that ours.

Carrots are always a good temptation, but I can stretch my neck a long way without moving my feet and she soon runs out of them. She is starting with the cajoling, then comes the swearing, and as she is feeling guilty the patting and even pleading, all the time I can see her frustration. After a while, which she says is nearly two hours, whatever that means, I am coming to the idea that I had better go in the trailer when another bossy person comes over with a clip board and tells my twarm that they will be closing the gates soon.

He just stands there clicking his ballpoint pen, being annoying. He is close enough to my rump for me to shuffle over a bit and knock into him. I notice my twarm trying to hide a smile as he drops his pen and must scrabble around for It.

Anne drives her lorry over, all loaded and ready for home. "Shall I try to get him in here, Di? I've only got Beau aboard and there's room for Nick."

So I get as much grass in my mouth as I can while Anne and my twarm open up the lorry.
"Oh, hi Beau, mind if I join you?"
"Be my guest, Nick."
My twarm with empty trailer is driving out of the field but stops at the gate. I hear the busy body say.
"Get him loaded them?"
"Nope," she said, "I'm leaving him here, you can have him. I'm going home for a large vodka."
I hear her laugh as she drives on.

Here we are, home again, and there is Di standing at my open stable door with my feed bucket in one hand and a glass in the other. The trailer? Already put away.

Lucida's Tale

by Claire Walker

'Twas up that secret turret stair that the Child did meet the Archivist.
"Boredom ails me; tell me your name," the flame-haired cherub said.
"I am Lamia, Child, and I'll tell you a tale," the Archivist replied,
"A tale of love and destiny."
And before her laid the open page.

*

Here's Lucida, a maiden fair, the tale began; an orphan, she:
For came marauding raptors from the North, and left her people slain;
All torn by iron claws and whipping swords.
Pursued by her own dead father, a revenant now, she readied Argent, the smith's white horse, and fled into the forest deep and Fae.
Brave Lucida! For many days she rode, watched by hidden Faerie eyes
In the eldritch dusk, and all but lured astray by giddy lights,
Or distant goblin music piping low.
A songbird followed, and she heard him often,
Lachrymal and sweetly pained, and wild and clear,
And she named him Oscen, the omen-bird.
And still she journeyed onwards - to where she did

not know,
Nor cared, in truth; her heart too sore to dwell beyond the here and now.
Then Oscen cried out loud and harsh - she saw it:
Though nought but a wisp, a fleeting shade
About the quaking aspens, a sylph, a sprite of air, mayhap;
But then a vision formed: white tresses lifted by a phantom breeze,
A cloak of cloudy silver, eyes of deepest amethyst,
And a moonstone, pale and pearly, at her throat.
No birds sang; no small creature scratched in the undergrowth;
All around was silence.
Until the woman - if thus she was - beckoned with a slender hand,
Then spake, her voice a keening on the air.
"Mulciber awaits thee, lady fair, and you must go,
Cross the Volcanic Lands, traverse the straits and rainy mountains
To lost and lonely Castle Maeror."
Lucida whirled and urged her steed away,
And Oscen cried again, that awful sound.
And on they rode,
Until she found her passage thwarted by a mile-high, mighty wall:
Her peregrinations were for nought, it seemed, but -
Mulciber awaits thee...
Compelled to trace its crinkle-crankle length, until

At last she found in those emphatic stones a breach. No forfeit paid,
She sallied forth, to lands of scorching heat and scouring winds,
And where, far off, black towers soared to prick the blood-red sky.
The Obsidian City: at first, she feared that hell;
But soon she found its vices pleased her well;
So well she might have stayed forever, but -
Mulciber awaits thee...
Plagued by demon-haunted, fevered dreams,
She donned new leather garments black, and boots with silver spurs,
And followed that siren call.
The perilous Straits of Doubt were broached on fearsome currents
That churned and roiled beneath their flimsy barque;
She fell ashore; and there - beheld the Imber Mountains.
Daunted, weary, she might have wept, but something called her onwards.
Mulciber awaits thee...
All was mist and moisture, and the din of cascades down the deep ravines,
And Argent's clop and slide on the rain-greased rocks.
'Til from the vale rose Maeror, in its lake of smoke and glass,
Despondent, dour, despairing 'neath its grievous

shroud of tears.
Wraith-like, those clouds that girt the sunless towers shadowed the bosky way;
Looming silhouettes of cypress flanked the roadway to the door.
Lucida crossed the empty threshold.
Her timid call unanswered, she ventured onwards,
Upwards, climbed the narrow spiral stair.
'Til at a latticed window, a large, dark figure slouched,
Defeat was in its shoulders, and its mien.
"You are Mulciber," she whispered, awed.
Alarmed, he rose, turned his glaucous gaze upon her -
She saw his fallen-angel face, and knew at once
That this was not some savage beast, or malefic fiend,
But a noble man, a prince imprisoned 'neath a dark enchantment.
"Tell me who you are, and whence you came," that prince demanded.
"I am Lucida," came her reply. "What fate befell you, that you suffer so?"
"A sorceress cursed me, when I could love her not.
She confined me to these walls and she took my sight,
That I may never look upon another. Only a kiss can set me free.
Will you kiss me, then?" he said, his sardonic words a lash

To Lucida's tender heart. "Sweet Lucida, wilt thou kiss me?"
So she upped and kissed him where he stood.
He jerked in shock, and gave a startled cry –
For his sight was restored, and his once-heavy heart was light.
Stunned, he gazed upon her, his eyes a cloudless summer sky;
He rained gentle kisses on her brow, and stroked back her flaming locks,
And said, "Marry me, sweet Lucida, and be my wife, my life."
So they were wed, and ever after dwelt in sunny idylls,
With Oscen's song, and woodlarks, and children's joyful laughter all around.

*

"A happy end!" the Child now cried with joy, "but the hour grows late,
And to supper I must go. So farewell, Archivist, lady Lamia, and many thanks!"
And the Child was gone.

The Archivist narrowed her amethyst eyes, and caressed her lambent stone.
She smoothed her tumbling snow-like tresses and shook her head.
"This is not the end," she said.

My Grandfather's Clock
by Helen Thwaites

Silent now the old clock stands,
Its heart no longer beating,
The song of its soul,
That rang out with such joy,
Is but a distant memory.

As a young child I would sit for hours and gaze at the painted figures dancing so joyfully in the idyllic country scene. The constant tick, tock, tick, tock, and the regular chiming, was not only like music, but to my childlike imagination seemed to be telling me so many stories. I would often say to grandfather that the clock had been talking to me, or I would tell him the story I had discovered that day.

As I got older, I began to write these stories down in a special book that grandfather bought me for my tenth birthday. I continued to do this for several years and in several books, always bought for me by grandfather, each year until I went away to university.

I can remember the first time I returned to grandfather's house after several months away. I had missed him so much, and felt so homesick, that my excitement at returning to this place of childhood happiness had been almost overwhelming. But as I entered the room where the old clock stood, the feeling of disappointment and realisation that I had grown up took over. Of course, the love I felt for my grandfather was as strong as ever, and my love of the old clock hadn't waned either. The disappointment I felt was in myself and my lack of imagination. I had never thought that I would lose this. No longer could I hear a story being told or a song being sung, just the constant tick, tock, tick, tock and regular chiming of the old clock. My special books still sat on the old bookshelf in my old room, but remained untouched, unopened and unloved for many years. In fact, I had almost forgotten they existed.

Silent now the old clock stands,
Its stories remain untold,
The song of its soul,
No longer resounds,
Oh, how I long to hear it once more.

Today I say my final goodbye to my grandfather. I can remember as a child thinking that this day would never come. He had always been here, been part of my life and now he has gone. I feel so lost. I haven't wanted to come back to this house since grandfather died nearly three weeks ago, but it seemed fitting that we all gather here today, so here I am. Glancing up at the old clock, an icy shiver pulses right through me. We had realised the clock had stopped working the day grandfather died, but it is only now I can see that its face is also looking sad. The lifeless hands are showing twenty-two minutes past seven, which was the very minute that grandfather's heart had stopped beating. For several minutes I stand frozen unable to take my eyes off the motionless hands. Only the sound of the doorbell ringing, telling us it is time to go, breaks my melancholic reverie, and I turn away, but that image of the sad clock face remains with me.

Silent now the old clock stands,
Its heart no longer beating,
The song of its soul,
That rang out with such joy,

Is but a distant memory.

***

At the reading of the will a few weeks later, I am given a small parcel wrapped in brown paper, and a small box. I untie the string and the paper falls away to reveal all my special books. He had kept them for me all these years! Tears prick at my eyes, but it is only as I open the box that they begin to flow. Inside is my grandfather's gold pocket watch and chain together with a tiny silver key. I know straight away what this is. He is giving me the clock. I am determined that the constant tick, tock, tick, tock and regular chiming of its heart and soul will once more be heard through a new house, and my own child will know their great grandfather through the stories that it tells.

Stolen by the Smog

by Helen Thwaites

The minutes went by so slowly that time itself seemed to be running down. The fading autumn light and thickening, choking yellow smog made the uninterrupted silence hard to bear. The grandfather clock in the hall began to strike.

"One, two, three, four, five, six."

Even the sound of my own hushed whisper couldn't cut through the ever-deepening sense of dread and fear that was filling my silence. She was not coming home. Coral had insisted on cycling to work that morning in spite of the smog warnings on the wireless. I had tried to persuade her to use the bus instead, but once she had set her mind on something, nothing was going to dissuade her.

I stood gazing out of the window in desperation, but even the light from the streetlamps could not penetrate through the thick yellow shroud that had fallen that night. The street was as silent as the room in which I stood and the atmosphere as sinister and solemn. A faint headlamp from a bicycle appeared to slow but kept going and silence returned once more. The route to Coral's place of work took her along beside the river and was never safe, but the smog gave cover to those who intended harm to the unwary and the river simply became invisible.

Again, the hall clock sounded its deep mournful notes and another hour had passed. Since my husband was taken from me in The Blitz at the beginning of 1941, my much younger sister had been my only companion. Frank and I had only been married eight months, so our plans for a family would never be more than a once longed-for dream. But when tragedy hit for a second time and our parents were killed only weeks after my Frank, Coral at only fifteen and myself at barely twenty-six clung to each other. This was twelve long years ago and seemed like another lifetime.

Now, here I was sitting alone of an evening again for the first time since Coral had come to live with me, and the dread of another tragedy unfolding was as real as it had been as the bombs rained down and another street was flattened. The only light in the room was the glow from the fire gently crackling in the hearth which I barely remember lighting, but I know I must have. Even the crackling from the fire sounded hollow and empty that night. At that moment nothing seemed real to me, and I could find no comfort in anything.

Time seemed to pass even more slowly as the evening faded into night. I decided to make my way to the hall and look at the clock as I hadn't heard it strike eight. I stood and stared in disbelief as the hands indicated only quarter past seven and it was definitely still working. I returned to the living room and turned on the light, but this only emphasised the silent emptiness of the house.

As my fear for Coral deepened I found myself becoming irritated too.

"If she has gone somewhere else with her friends in this weather I'll, I'll..."

I stopped myself and giggled at the irony of what I had been about to say, in spite of how I was feeling.

Coral was no longer the thoughtless, somewhat irresponsible teenager; she was a grown woman with a life and ideas of her own. Quite often recently, it had been her who had shown the common sense, maturity and stability expected of people of our ages more than me. A cold shiver ran right through me and I knew at that moment something had happened to her.

With no telephone at home, I decided that I had no choice but to try and make my way to a telephone box and call the police. I had not been walking long before the heavy smog caused me to become disorientated and began to make me breathless. I knew that I could go no further and with a heavy heart I turned back and prayed that I could at least find my way home.

That night was the longest of my life and the only thing I could think was that my one remaining light in this struggling world had been stolen by the smog.

The following morning the smog still clung stubbornly and menacingly to the river and surrounding streets. Even in areas where it had begun to clear the pungent stench of sulphur lingered and daylight was thickly veiled.

With my heart pounding and an ever-deepening sense of dread I made my way towards the police station. On my arrival I was met with a scene of utter chaos. So many people trying to get information, report incidents or waiting to receive news. I knew straight away that I would have a long wait ahead. Frantic people continued to arrive in ever increasing numbers, and those already waiting continued to wait, and in turn, receive news or information often only confirming their worst fears, or else telling them nothing at all.

I began to wonder whether I would rather know for sure or remain in ignorance. Perhaps not knowing would have allowed me to keep at least a flicker of hope alive, however small that flicker may have been. Then it happened. A young sergeant rushed in carrying a lady's bag. My heart lurched and I crumpled onto the floor. It was Coral's bag. Another young officer who had been trying to maintain some order amidst the increasing frustration and desperation-fuelled chaos came to my aid and helped me to a chair.

"Are you alright, Madam? Did you recognise that bag?"

Unable to speak, I simply nodded my head and then the tears refused to be held back any longer.

"All right, Madam, I will speak to the sergeant and see what I can find out for you."

The tears continued to fall as I sat and stared into space, no longer aware of the chaos. I was numb. By the time the second officer returned, accompanied by the young sergeant, I had lost all concept of how much time had passed. But I had recovered my ability to speak.

“Please, Sergeant, can you tell me where the bag was found? I must know! You see, it belongs to my sister who never returned home from work last night and I am out of my mind with worry. I must know what has happened to her! I need to find out if she is all right. Please, tell me what you know.’

“All right, madam, all in good time. First, we need some basic details. Will you allow me to help you into a side room where we can talk privately and without interruption?”

My heart lurched in my chest for the second time that day as the door of the small dimly lit room had closed behind me. I felt trapped but knew that was the only way I was going to find the answers I so desperately needed.

“Right, please take your time and try to tell me as much as you can. Let’s start by taking your name, shall we?”

“Beryl, Beryl Matthews.”

“Thank you, Mrs Matthews. Now, can you tell me your sister’s name and a bit about what brought you here today?”

My voice faltered and my throat tightened as I related the details of the preceding day and night. The more I said, the more serious the expression on the face of the sergeant became, and the less I wanted to know. Once I had told him everything I could, there was an uncomfortably long pause while the sergeant and a constable who had also been listening conferred between them.

"Thank you, Mrs Matthews, you have been very thorough, everything you have told us has been a great help. We do understand how difficult this time of uncertainty must have been, and I fear the next few minutes are not going to make things any easier for you. I am sorry, but a bicycle has been found only a few yards from where I discovered your sister's bag, and we need to know if it is hers, but unfortunately as yet we have no news of your sister."

By the time I left the police station, I felt confused, numb and void of hope. The bag was Coral's, but the bicycle was not. It was as though every other sign of her had completely vanished. I also discovered that she had never made it to work the previous morning so had been missing for far longer than I first believed.

The house felt even more empty than when I had left only a few hours earlier. Another day faded into evening with the hollow crackle from the fire and the mournful chime from the clock the only sounds to break the desolate silence.

***

My life stopped that night. I simply went on existing until I heard that the case of my sister's disappearance was to be scaled down and stopped unless some new evidence could be found. This was six months after she had vanished and even her bicycle remained unfound. My desperation for answers reawakened a passion within me and I pleaded with the police to keep looking. It was at that point I discovered three other young women had also been lost that fateful day and no evidence had been found of them at all. Surely these four disappearances were connected? Was there another link between these four young women? Did they know each other? Something had happened and there had to be some answers somewhere.

Later that week two bodies were found by the mud larks on the banks of the Thames. Neither of them was Coral, but it meant the cases remained open. The remains of a third young woman were found by the mudlarks a week later. The coroner confirmed drowning as the cause of death in all three cases but could not say whether it had been accidental or murder.

***

To this day Coral's case remains unsolved, but I cannot comprehend how anybody can simply disappear without trace. Has my one remaining light in this struggling world truly been stolen by the smog?

Full Circle

by Ray Breach

Professor Lefevre pushed the leather key fob across the desk towards the dark-haired young woman sitting opposite.

"It's your one chance for freedom, Celine, take it."

The Sorbonne had been awash with gossip about the two of them throughout her final year as a medical student. Now, on the very cusp of her qualification, the war had intervened in the most dramatic way possible.

"But Uncle Charles..."

They had kept their familial relationship secret, more worried that her brilliance would be ascribed to nepotism, preferring to risk something potentially far more scandalous.

He slid back the garage doors to reveal the gleaming black Citroen, not yet a year old.

"The tank is full and there are three more cans in the boot. Drive at seventy kilometres an hour, that way she will cover fifteen kilometres on a litre. Oh, and don't forget to freewheel down the hills. You should easily make Marseille."

There were still two of hours of daylight remaining when she reached the obelisk at Fontainbleu. Charles had expressly told her to stop for nobody, but the young man in RAF uniform seemed a safe enough passenger.

She looked at the streak of dried blood on his left temple as he swung into the seat beside her.

“It's nothing, I caught it on the edge of the canopy. I was in a hurry to get out of my burning Spitfire. Like a damned fool I followed the Stuka down and then saw the infantry column. I was using up the rest of my ammunition on them when a bullet hit my radiator. Won't this thing go any faster?”

Celine chuckled “It's a Citroen, not a Spitfire.”

She explained that she was heading for Marseille and their sedate progress was to conserve fuel. Just before Lyon the gauge nudged empty. They pulled over and Sergeant Bob Griffin decanted thirty litres of petrol into the tank.

“Reminds me of being at home.” He explained that his father ran a small garage in a South Downs village.

They left the Citroen on the Marseille waterfront. The S.S. Bracklyn had been built in the last decade of the previous century. She was an ugly salt-caked hulk that appeared to be held together by rust and plied a regular route between Marseille and Liverpool. Her holds were already filled with bauxite ore that was mined in Provence.

The crew welcomed them aboard. Wung Lo watched carefully as the needle on the boiler pressure gauge climbed towards the point where he would release the steam, turning the propellor that would drive the Bracklyn at a leisurely twelve knots. He motioned to Felipe, the young Spanish stoker, that the boiler had enough coal. The young veteran of the Spanish Civil War was already covered from head to toe in black dust.

Wung Lo pulled the stopper from the brass voice pipe and spoke into it in an accent that came from somewhere between Shanghai and Liverpool. "OK, Soft Lad, take her away."

On the bridge Captain Herbert Fazackerley DSO tapped out his pipe on the compass binnacle and refilled it. He smiled at the engineer's unintentional irreverence. The mischievous Scouse cook who he had learned the expression from had taught Wung Lo that it was the highest term of respect, only to be used when addressing one's superiors or high-ranking officials. Oh, and of course, police officers. The easy going Fazackerley had never bothered to correct him on this false piece of etiquette.

Wung Lo had proved to be a mechanical genius who had managed to keep the decrepit vessel steaming despite the fact that the half century old ship was disintegrating around him. His collection of old tea chests in the corner of the engine room contained all manner of bits and bobs that enabled him to bodge a leaking pipe or a blown gasket to allow them to steam, or at least limp, into port for a more permanent repair. Their voyage through the Straits of Gibraltar and across the Bay of Biscay took eight days. On the platform at Lime Street station Celine slipped Bob the piece of paper with her address scrawled on it as they went their separate ways.

In July 1940 leafy North Oxford seemed a million miles from the war. Aunt Amelie had married Claud after meeting in Paris shortly after the last war. He was a surgeon at St. Hugh's, now a specialist hospital for head injuries. The college had been requisitioned and, since Dunkirk, was overrun with patients.

Their rambling ivy clad Victorian house off the Banbury Road had become a meeting place for an eclectic mix of people. Academics, bohemians, medics and Claud's old army colleagues could be found seated around the huge refectory table most nights. They discussed all manner of subjects, their conversation lubricated by copious amounts of wine.

On the last Saturday in July, Celine found herself seated next to a tall moustachioed man in the considerably less than immaculate uniform of a Colonel. Athelny "Stinker" Chapman explained that he had been at school with Claud. He inserted a black Sobranie into a long cigarette holder and lit it with a gold lighter, ostentatiously embossed with his initials. At the end of the evening he took a business card from his cigarette case and handed it to Celine.

“If you fancy an interesting job look me up some time.”

She saw that the address on the card was Baker Street in London.

Bob Griffin came to visit the following weekend. He had three days leave and had driven up from the aerodrome in Kent. They agreed to meet again when he next got leave, although, as he explained, things were hotting up.

When she had not heard from him after a fortnight, she managed to get through to a number he had given her. The man who answered was a member of his squadron. “I'm sorry. Griffo went missing the day before yesterday. He hit a Messerschmitt and chased him out across The Channel. We are told not to do it, but it happens. We've heard nothing."

The following morning Celine put a call through to Chapman. She took the train into London and made her way to his office in Baker Street. Athelny Chapman blew a long plume of cigarette smoke towards the nicotine-stained ceiling.

"What would you say to going back to France?"

The first Wednesday of January had been quiet in the emergency department of the Radcliffe Infirmary. It was a pleasant contrast with the chaos of the previous few days, the drunks, the fights and car crashes that had accompanied the holiday period now gone. Doctor Celine Griffin browsed the newspaper over a coffee. She was confronted with a picture of the twisted wreckage of an expensive French sports car. The headline was 'Albert Camus Dead'. The famous French author and philosopher had accepted a lift with his publisher, despite having a train ticket in his pocket. On the Route Nationale south of Paris the car had left the road at high speed with devastating results.

Celine quickly turned the page. Six weeks earlier, on a foggy November night in a denouement that was heavily laden with irony, Bob Griffin had crashed his Jaguar into, of all vehicles, a brewery lorry, on the outskirts of Oxford. He had died instantly when the impact had driven the steering column through his chest. She recalled his conversation with the salesman who had counselled caution in driving such a powerful car.

“I flew a Spitfire,” countered Bob.

He had always been a man possessed of more confidence than competence. A confidence only increased by his excessive consumption of the products of the very brewery that owned the lorry. In Bob's view if he could still stand then he could still drive perfectly well.

At the funeral Celine had got into a long conversation with Tom. She had always found it difficult to believe that they were brothers, so different in every way. She recalled the dinner party when Bob had been talking about his wartime exploits that had ended abruptly on the beach at Calais, his engine blown apart after using the boost for three full minutes in a vain attempt to catch the fleeing Messerschmitt that would have been his fifth kill, confirming him as an ace. Paradoxically there was no doubt in Celine's mind that this mad pursuit had saved his life.

Tom had pointedly asked Celine about her war.

“Not much to tell, really.”

But Tom had persisted with his questioning, teasing from the reluctant heroine a few scant details about her three years as an SOE agent while her husband to be had cooled his heels in a prisoner of war camp. Bob had resented the shift of focus to his wife as her fascinated guests had prised those anecdotes from her, like oysters from their shells.

Tom, two years younger than his brother, a quiet unassuming solicitor, had married the office typist. It had been a mismatch of Bob and Celine proportions. The glamorous blonde with her narrow waist and stiletto heels had stayed with him for two years before a private investigator had set up the meeting in a Brighton hotel room to instigate their divorce.

The Aldermaston March that Tom had persuaded Celine to accompany him on had been the catalyst to their relationship. Over that first Easter of the new decade, in the company of students, beatniks, batty old ladies and colonels who thought that the H bomb wasn't quite cricket and that wars should be decided by cavalry charges, the couple wended their weary way over the fifty-two miles. The protestors had arrived in Trafalgar Square forty thousand strong. Tom had proposed later that evening in the intimate little Soho restaurant by the light of candles in Chianti bottles.

When their daughter Lucie arrived the following spring, the couple discussed the possibility of making a fresh start. The presbytery in the village just outside Bayeux where Celine had grown up charmed them. The rambling old building with the apple orchard behind was their dream, the price ridiculously low. The obvious drawback, a gaping hole in the gable end where a seventeen-pounder shell from a Sherman Firefly had abruptly ended the career of a Nazi sniper on D Day.

Tom set to work on the renovations along with a couple of local builders while Celine worked in the hospital in the picturesque Norman city. Once the work was completed Tom decided upon a change of direction. Scouring the brocante shops and flea markets he bought up all manner of artefacts and domestic knickknacks. He had a talent for finding pieces that appealed to a growing market. Once a month he hitched the trailer to his big Citroen estate and took the ferry from Cherbourg. At holiday times Lucie sat in the back, singing along to the radio, her favourite song featuring newspaper taxis that appeared on the shore. She was convinced that it had been written for her.

Their destination once ashore was a small antique shop in The Lanes in Brighton. Tom's younger sister Eloise, a distinctly bohemian girl, and her partner Bill, a lady with a penchant for corduroy trousers and brogues, fell like locusts on the eagerly awaited consignments. Their shop became a place popular with couples seeking to bring a hint of the flavour of rural France to their suburban homes. As his contacts grew Tom branched out and the business grew. He acquired a lorry and began exporting provincial furniture, unwanted in France but the talking point of many swish British dinner parties.

Lucie was a bright girl who took all the academic hurdles without breaking her stride. The interview at St.Hugh's in Oxford was a formality. One member of the panel suspected the identity of her mother but nepotism was never going to be needed for her to gain a place. It was only when they met again at the tutorial in her first term that he posed the question.

“Are you any relation to Celine Griffin?”

Lucie Bannerman and Dominique Aubert sat in the shade of an apple tree in the orchard behind the old presbytery where they had first played as children a half century earlier. Their careers, although both in medicine, had followed very different trajectories. Lucie, specialising in neurosurgery, had become one of the foremost experts in her field, her friend a modest country doctor.

The sun was lower now, the golden evening rays

slanting through the tree branches, heavily laden with fruit as autumn approached.

Dominique pointed to the dark wooden cross over by the house wall.

“A pet?”

“Oh, that's Fritz the Boche. That is how dad always referred to him. They dug him up when they were building the garage. It was just after I had left for Oxford. There was identification on him, and dad contacted his brother. They were happy to leave him here where he died. There was no other family, his wife and child were killed in an air raid shortly before the war ended.”

They went on to discuss the extraordinary events that had accompanied the commemoration of the sixtieth anniversary of D Day.

“Yes, it all began when this Martin Pontier got talking to a journalist.”

Lucie had found it difficult to comprehend that the man with the wild red hair pictured in the newspaper, bandoliers slung across his shoulder, Bren gun casually held at his side, was now this retired Boulogne notary, cigarette ash in the folds of his voluminous waistcoat, carpet-slippered from repeated attacks of the gout.

The article had focused on how the resistance group had attacked the German troop train, the dynamited track responsible for the derailment, followed by the crash down the embankment that had resulted in many casualties.

The story was then syndicated into Germany where Helmut Dressler, a retired Berlin businessman, watched it on the evening news. His mind went back to the sultry July night in nineteen-forty-four, his prosthetic left arm a lifelong reminder of the terror that had befallen his regiment.

Dressler, now seventy-eight years old, nudged his wife. “That was the train I was on.”

Three weeks later the cameras in the Paris television studio panned around the audience before settling on the presenter as the music introduced the nightly current affairs program.

The two women had gone inside the house, the thick walls of pale stone keeping the building cool even in summer. Lucie slipped the disc into the television and the screen came to life showing the three elderly guests facing the cameras as Lucie explained the background to the story to her friend.

Celine Griffin, neatly dressed and immaculately coiffured in a manner that belied her eighty-seven years, challenged Pontier about his placing of the explosives. The small charge had been designed to merely derail the train, but instead the Resistance fighter had placed it under the rail beside the steep drop that had caused the carriages to roll over causing the extensive casualties.

Pontier responded curtly. "It was war. We had been occupied for more than four years. It was justified."

Dressler extended a hand and placed it on Celine's forearm. He shook his head as if to admonish her for the intervention.

"He is quite correct of course. And I will always be grateful for what he did."

The interviewer looked puzzled at this and he addressed the German. "Would you like to explain that?"

Dressler took a drink from his water glass and continued in good but heavily accented French.

"My regiment was being transported to the front. The first train had more than a thousand men, ours a similar number. Do you know how many survived the war?" He answered his own question.

"It was seventeen. They were ordered not to retreat. They called it The Cauldron, you know. All of my comrades, many no older than boys, were trapped in those high banked lanes. The allied aircraft went up and down firing their rockets and cannon until the regiment was virtually annihilated. Then most of the survivors were killed before the war finally ended. Fighting a war that was already lost. Only those either taken prisoner or injured like me went on to have a full life."

He continued. "So maybe, Madame, don't be too harsh on Monsieur Pontier. He was fighting his own war in his own way."

He tapped his left arm with his right hand. "And this is what saved me. Those who had survived the crash unscathed were then forced to fight that terrible battle. Then they went on to defend Germany. Of course, with only one arm there was little I could do. It was that injury that bought me sixty more years."

Dominique picked up her briefcase. "I had better go, I have a couple more calls to make. It's been good meeting up again. Maybe we won't leave it so long, neither of us are youngsters anymore."

She opened her briefcase. "I will leave these here."

She placed a sheaf of papers on the kitchen table.

“You will need these to register your mother's death at the Mairie, there are copies for the notary and the undertaker too."

Lucie walked out to the car with her friend. “I found some letters amongst her private possessions.”

“What sort of letters?”

“They were written by Martin Pontier. From reading them I think that they must have been more than comrades.”

About the Authors

Claire Walker
Originally from Manchester, Claire has finally found her spiritual home in Suffolk. When not writing or working as a librarian, she enjoys walking on her local beach and practising yoga where she is determined to master the headstand.

Ivan Whomes
Ivan was born in this coastal town and has loved books since belonging to the Lowestoft Borough Junior Library. As well as stories, Ivan also writes songs which he has been known to perform on his piano accordion.

Midge Mellor
A hippie at heart, Midge enjoys living in the countryside. She loves animals and her little dog, Bo, is always by her side, on her lap or sitting at her feet. Story writing and storytelling are her passions.

Helen Thwaites
A Christian with a great love of nature, Helen takes most of her inspiration from these aspects of her life. As well as writing historical fiction and poetry, she enjoys many handicrafts and musical theatre.

Di Bettinson
Getting older is such fun. Di, now retired, enjoys acting, painting (on paper, not walls) and, of course, writing. In between, comes walking with her big dog.

Hilary Lepine
Hilary lives a stone's throw from Pakefield beach, a favourite place where daily she can walk her dogs, and muse. Under her pen name of Lottie Thorn, she has published children's books in her "Mabel" series. She is currently completing a novel.

Ray Breach
A frustrated journalist, I spent forty years selling second-hand cars before discovering the Pakefield Writing Group. Interests: reading, writing, politics and travel. One regret: I never played centre forward for the Netherlands. As a consolation, I have a cat named Mr Orange.

About Pakefield Writing Group

The Pakefield Writing Group was born in March 2019. Initially meeting monthly, the seven members of the group wanted to meet once a week during the pandemic lockdown to keep their minds active. The group still meets weekly, honing their skills, with each member of the group producing a story every month.

Printed in Great Britain
by Amazon

20477962R00078